arr: A favorite pirate expression used to show anger, sadness, or happiness.

hearties: Loyal workers.

TE TALK

Shiver me timbers: "This is surprising!"

scuttle-butt: A gossip; someone who spreads rumors.

sea dog: An experienced pirate.

BAD PIRATE

Written by
Kari-Lynn Winters

pajamapress

Illustrated by
Dean Griffiths

First published in the United States in 2015

This is a first edition.

10 9 8 7 6 5 4 3 2 1

www.pajamapress.ca info@pajamapress.ca

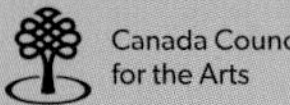

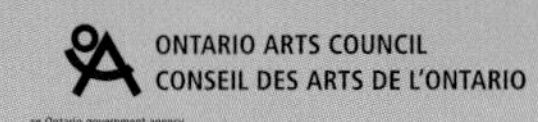

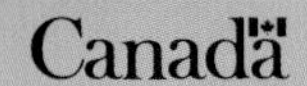

The publisher gratefully acknowledges the support of the Canada Council for the Arts and the Ontario Arts Council for its publishing program. We acknowledge the financial support of the Government of Canada through the Canada Book Fund (CBF) for our publishing activities.

Library and Archives Canada Cataloguing in Publication

Winters, Kari-Lynn, 1969-, author Bad pirate / written by Kari-Lynn Winters ; illustrated by Dean Griffiths.

ISBN 978-1-927485-71-2 (bound)

I. Griffiths, Dean, 1967-, illustrator II. Title.

PS8645.I5745B33 2015 jC813'.6 C2014-906878-6

Publisher Cataloging-in-Publication Data (U.S.)

Winters, Kari-Lynn, 1969-

Bad pirate / Kari-Lynn Winters ; Dean Griffiths.

[32] pages : color illustrations ; cm.

Summary: Her pirate captain father reminds her to be bold and saucy and selfish, but Augusta can't help being shy, polite, and helpful; in short, a bad pirate. But when a terrible storm puts the crew in danger, Augusta is bold enough to be true to herself and show that a good pirate can be selfless, too.

ISBN-13: 978-1-92748-571-2

1. Pirates – Juvenile fiction. 2. Fathers and daughters – Juvenile fiction. 3. Values – Juvenile fiction. I. Griffiths, Dean, 1967- . II. Title.

[E] dc23 PZ7.W458Ba 2015

Edited by Ann Featherstone
Designed by Rebecca Bender

Manufactured by Sheck Wah Tong Printing Ltd.
Printed in Hong Kong, China

Pajama Press Inc.
181 Carlaw Ave. Suite 207 Toronto, Ontario Canada, M4M 2S1

Distributed in Canada by UTP Distribution
5201 Dufferin Street Toronto, Ontario Canada, M3H 5T8

Distributed in the U.S. by Ingram Publisher Services
1 Ingram Blvd. La Vergne, TN 37086, USA

To me writing hearties, who are selfless and never bark orders: Ann Featherstone, Lisa Dalrymple, Aimee Reid, Rob Sanders, Ali McDonald, Alma Fullerton, Peggy Collins, Val Coulman, Brian Cretney, and to the students at Alder Park.

–KL.W.

For my own Wee Augusta, helpful shipmates John and Rebecca, and brave navigator Ann.

–D.G.

Captain Barnacle Garrick was **bad natured** and **horrible**, which most pirates would say was good—

very good.

Augusta Garrick was **good natured** and **helpful**, which most pirates would say was bad—

very bad.

Barnacle pulled his daughter aside.

To be a good pirate, yez gots to be **saucy.**

Aye!

And yez gots to be **bold.**

Aye!

But most important, me sea pup, yez gots to be SELFISH!
Um..., Papa?
Land ahoy...! Methinks.
Augusta couldn't stop herself. She adjusted the scope so her father could see the island better.

That afternoon, Augusta noticed a small tear in the mainsail.

She took the sewing kit, snuck up the mast, and secretly began to patch the sail.

Barnacle growled a warning.

Augusta scurried down to await her punishment.

But her father charged past her, barking at Squid and Bones.

Barnacle called an emergency meeting.
On this ship yez gots to be saucy.
Aye!
Aye!
Aye!
Aye!
Aye!
And yez gots to be bold.
Aye!
Aye!
Aye!

Every last sea dog cheered, except for one.

Scully gave Augusta a long and suspicious stare.

Yez better be makin' surez of it!
If I find a kindhearted
matey on board, yez be the one
feedin' the fishes!

That night, as Augusta tucked extra blankets around the shivering crew, she decided it was time to make her father proud.

She had to do something **selfish!**

Then, with one saucy, bold, and selfish move, she grabbed Scully's peg leg and threw it out the porthole.

Augusta felt seasick.
What had she done?
All night long she
tossed and turned.
Poor one-eyed Scully!

By morning a storm was brewing. Captain Garrick yelled from the poop deck.

Augusta found Scully.
The ship's sinking!
You need to mend the sail.
I can't findz me leg.
I'll help you.
Scully pushed her aside.
Helpz me?
I don't needz the help of a kindhearted lass!

Scully, man the sails!

Scully plopped onto his bunk.

Augusta jumped into action. With the speed of a cannonball, she found the sewing kit and scurried to the quarterdeck.

The ship's listin',
SCULLLLY!
The ship's sinkin'.
Save ye-selves!

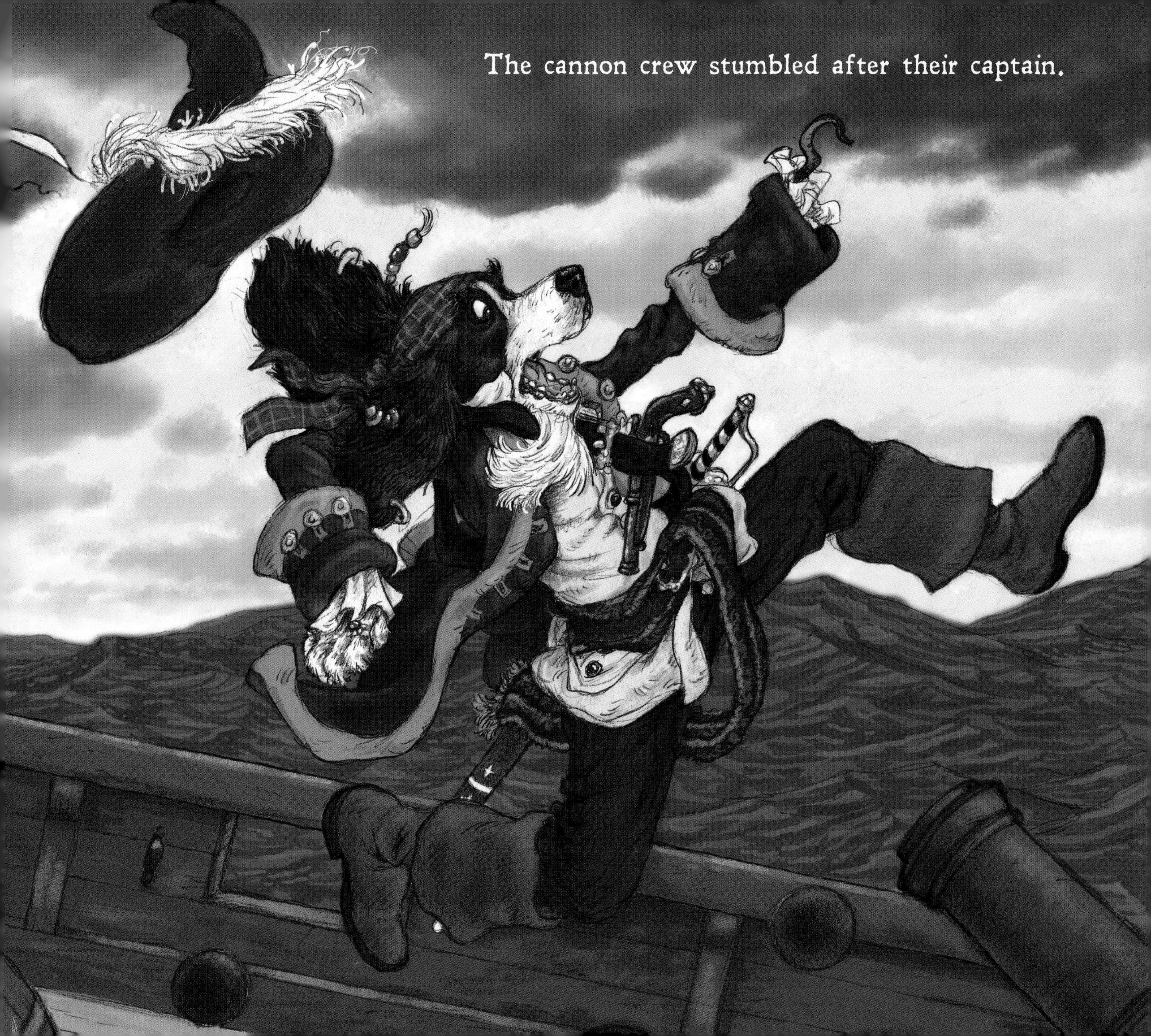

The cannon crew stumbled after their captain.

Barnacle snarled.
Whyz you have that kit?
That's not yer job!

Augusta grabbed his beard and pulled him close.

Her father patted her on the shoulder.

Augusta climbed the rigging.
Barnacle pointed.

But most important, me young lass,
yez gots to be self—

For the first time,
Augusta took charge.
Less speed!
Lads, help me reef the sails!

Barnacle cupped his ear.

Scully muttered,

Oh? Hmmm...
me thoughts exactly!
Lads, listen to me
sea-dog daughter!
Helmsman,
heave to!

As the ship steadied, Augusta climbed down.
The crewmembers fist-pumped a salute to her.

Barnacle hugged his girl.

And Augusta flashed her widest, scurviest smile.

A.G

bilge: The smelliest, dirtiest, and bottom-most part of the ship.

listin': Leaning to the side.

rigging: The lines and masts on sailing ships.

NAUTICAL

Land ahoy: "I see land over there!"

poop deck: The highest deck of a ship, located at the back.

heave to: Steer so that the wind no longer fills the sails and the ship stops moving forward.